EBELE BRIGHT

To my bold and fearless
daughters,

Neriah and Adira Bright

Love, mummy

Mama eagle is soaring the skies. Her little eaglets excitedly singing, "To the left, NOW to the right, go on straight. WOOHOO".

All but one, Chico!

"Chico, all your brothers are flying, it's your turn," said mama eagle flapping her wings in front of the nest.

"C'MON Chico!" adds Nico peaking in. "You can do this".

"I'm SC-A-ARED," stuttered Chico.

"You said that YESTERDAY, AND the day before, AND the week before!" teased Nico.

"Shhh Nico, off you go", said mama eagle.

Chico your wings are AWESOME, and your talons STRONG. You are a SUPER DUPER eaglet," said mama eagle wiggling.

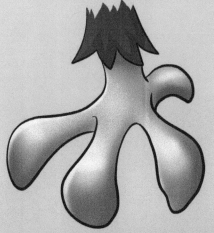

"You are built to soar the skies, and ZOOM ZOOM ZOOM, above the clouds," smiled mama eagle.

"What if I can't see where I'm going?" asked Chico.

"You are an eagle, and eagles have perfect vision," said mama eagle.

"What if I get caught in a storm mama?" asked Chico.

"You are an eagle! Eagles love storms, we fly even higher using the winds of the storm," said mama eagle.

"What if I fall?" asked Chico.

"You are an eagle, your wings are made not just to fly, but to SOAR. You just have to begin," said mama eagle.

"Oh mama, I'm SCARED. I've NEVER flown before!" cried Chico.

"Move in, I'll tell you about a VERY BRAVE eaglet who had never flown before. She was SO SCARED," said mama eagle.

"What did she do?" asked Chico eagerly.

"SNIFFLE! She CRIED, AND she CRIED, as she watched her sisters fly," said mama eagle.

"Oh, poor eaglet!" said Chico teary eyed.

"One day, she had enough of staying in the nest watching everybody else play," stood mama eagle.

"Really?" asked Chico wide eyed.

"Oh yes! She breathed in, OOO, and out, HAAA, and trusted her mama to throw her out of the nest, SWOOSH!" said mama eagle.

"AAAAHHHH!" gasped Chico.

"She FLAPPED and FLAPPED her wings, but she didn't take flight," whispered mama eagle.

"OH NO! What happened mama?" asked Chico.

"Well, her mama didn't let her fall. She caught her," said mama eagle.

"They tried over and over until one day, she rose higher and higher and her eyes met her mama's," she continued.

"SHE DID IT! She FLEW! I was that eaglet," said mama eagle.

"REALLY mama, YOU!" said Chico. "Yes really!" smiled mama eagle.

"But, but, YOU are the MOST incredible at flying," replied Chico.

"That's because I believed I could fly even though I was scared". "Always remember, you are bold, brave and fearless", said mama eagle.

"Okay mama, here I go," said Chico, a little nervous, but pretty excited.

"FLY CHICO FLY," he heard his brothers sing.

"AGAIN", screamed Chico. "AND AGAIN," laughed Chico, until he rose higher and higher, and his eyes met his mama's.

' **Always remember,
you are brave, bold
and fearless.** '

Ebele Bright

Announce World Publishing

Published in 2022 by Announce World publishing
Announce World Publishing is a trademark name for Announce World Ltd.
www.announceworld.com

First Edition

British Library Cataloguing in Publication Data:
A catalogue record for this book is available from the British Library.

ISBN 978-1-8382947-0-0 Hardback
ISBN 978-1-8382947-1-7 Paperback

Ingram Content Group UK Ltd.
Milton Keynes UK
UKHW050857260723
425760UK00004B/87